ARTHUR
THE LEGEND

STORY
DAVID CHAUVEL
DRAWING
JÉRÔME LERECULEY
COLOUR
JEAN-LUC SIMON

ENGLISH ADAPTATION
LANNIG TRESEIZH

With the demise of the Roman Empire, western Europe descended into the turmoil of the Dark Ages. However, with the end of Roman rule in Britain the island experienced a resurgence in the pre-invasion culture of its native inhabitants. It was the age of saints and poets, the time when the legendary figure of Arthur rose to prominence.

Known as the British Heroic Age, the cultural landscape of Britain had not yet experienced English domination. Britain was a Celtic island and the language of most of its inhabitants was Brythonic, which was soon to evolve into what we know today as Welsh and its sister languages Cornish and Breton.

The story presented in *Arthur: The Legend* derives from historical, mythological and poetic traditions compiled in ancient manuscripts such as the *Historia Brittonum*, the *Annales Cambriae*, the collection of fables known as the *Mabinogi* and numerous other ancient documents. This was a time long before the legends surrounding Arthur were appropriated, romanticized and spread across Europe by the Normans during the Middle Ages.

Britain as we know it today had yet to evolve. The island's division into England, Scotland and Wales had yet to happen. The English – or Saxons – had only begun to arrive in Britain. Scotland had not yet developed its Gaelic culture; its highlands were inhabited by the Picts, its lowlands by the Britons – indeed the oldest extant Welsh poetry was composed in praise of the Brythonic tribe of the Votadini who inhabited the region around modern-day Edinburgh.

It is into this context that we place *Arthur: The Legend*. The reader will consequently encounter personal and place names that may look alien and unpronounceable, but which reflect the original names found in the sources. They are presented in this graphic novel in their modern orthographic form, with a pronunciation reference at the end of the book, and are a fascinating insight into the most ancient references to the enigmatic character of Arthur.

ARTHUR THE LEGEND

BOOK 1

MYRDDIN

WILD MAN OF THE WOODS

People & Places

CYMRY means 'compatriots', and is the modern Welsh designation for the people of Wales. 'Cymry' and **BRYTHON** are often transposed in the early sources as the people they refer to are identical. To avoid confusion with the modern usage of 'Briton', 'Brython' is used throughout this book.

ISLE OF THE MIGHTY is the romantic name for Britain, reflecting the stature of its inhabitants. Its northernmost headland called **BALAWON**, its southernmost point called **PENWEDD**. The mountain range of **ERYRI** is Snowdonia in Wales.

GWRTHEYRN is Welsh form of Vortigern, meaning 'high king'. The name is possibly an honorific title given to the Chief of the Lords of Britain. The monk Gildas, in his *De Excidio et Conquestu Britanniae*, refers to Vortigern as the 'superbus tyrannus', or proud tyrant.

PICTS, the inhabitants of the highlands of modern Scotland. Historical adversaries of the Brythons, their culture may have been very similar. **GOIDELS** and **GAELS** are both terms relating to the **IRISH**, at times adversaries and allies of the Brythons.

CYSTENNIN FYCHAN, known as Constans in the sources, he stood in Vortigern's way to becoming Chief of the Lords of Britain.

HENGEST, the legendary leader of the Saxon advent to Britain. In reality, he could have been a Saxon god figure. His base was **CAER Y GARRAI**, meaning 'fort of the twine', traditionally the first Saxon foothold in Britain, yielded by Gwrtheyrn. Hengest's most malevolent deed was the **TREACHERY OF THE LONG KNIVES**, the plot to murder 300 Brython nobles during a feast given in their honour. **EIDOL** of Caerloyw (Gloucester) was only one of two Brythons to escape with their lives.

MYRDDIN is the original Welsh name for Merlin. Early manuscripts refer to two characters called Myrddin, their traditions intertwined over the centuries. The first was the poet Myrddin Wyllt ('the Wild' or 'Mad'), also known as Llallogan (Lailoken) who exiled himself to the Forest of Celyddon. The second was a character closely associated with the tales of Emrys Wledig. According to Geoffrey of Monmouth's *Vita Merlini*, Myrddin was married to **GWENDDOLEN**, sister of king **RHYDDERCH HAEL** (the Generous) of Ystrad Clud (Strathclyde).

MORFRYN FRYCH, according to the *Red Book of Hergest*, was the father of Myrddin and his sister **GWENDDYDD**, wife to Rhydderch Hael. Her discourse with her brother is central to the prophetic poem *The Dialogue of Myrddin and his sister Gwenddydd*.

CERIDWEN; ancient tradition surrounding Ceridwen associates her with a magic cauldron of learning. She had three children, including her vacuous son **AFAGDDU**, for whom she prepared a potion of muse and wisdom. The three magic drops destined for Afagddu were instead consumed by the hapless **GWION BACH** who, filled with knowledge and learning, later became the bard **TALIESIN**, destined to grow into one of the major poets of the early Welsh tradition.

BLODEUWEDD was the mythological wife created from flowers for Lleu Llaw Gyffes by the magician Gwydion.

EMRYS WLEDIG, associated with the historical Romano-British figure Ambrosius Aurelianus who was successful in battle against the Saxons. 'Gwledig' is the title given to warleaders in post-Roman Britain.

GWYNNYS, the location of Gwrtheyrn's fortress, is lost in a plethora of different traditions. The historian Nennius says Gwrtheyrn built his fort in 'Guunnessi', possibly the secluded coastal valley of Nant Gwrtheyrn in north Wales.

THE FOREST OF CELYDDON was a vast forest stretching across the lowlands of modern-day Scotland (or the 'Old North' in Welsh tradition) and which is the root of 'Caledonia'.

THE GIANT'S DANCE, according to tradition the stones of Stonehenge originated in Ireland, relocated to Britain by Myrddin, and aligned with the sunrise of the summer solstice, or **ALBAN HEFIN**.

GWYNDDOLAU was a chieftain from the Old North with a hunger for land. Defeated in the battle of **ARFDERYDD** in the year 573, where Myrddin was gripped by madness. In a divergence from the sources, this book links Myrddin with Rhydderch Hael; the old poems tell us Myrddin was a member of Gwynddolau's court, persecuted by Rhydderch in the Forest of Celyddon after the battle.

BEFORE HIS APPOINTMENT, GWRTHEYRN WAS OPPOSED BY ANOTHER WORTHY CHIEFTAIN, THE PRINCE CYSTENNIN FYCHAN.

GWRTHEYRN HAD UNDER HIS COMMAND A FORCE OF VIOLENT PICTS, WARRIORS LOYAL ONLY TO HIM, WITH A PROMISE OF A PORTION OF THE SPOILS UPON DEFEAT OF THE SAXONS.

EVER WILLING TO SUBMIT TO DECEIT IN ORDER TO ATTAIN HIS POSITION AS HIGH KING, GWRTHEYRN COMMANDED HIS PICTISH FORCE TO KILL HIS RIVAL.

BUT WHEN THE PICTS CAME TO CLAIM THEIR REWARD, THEIR HANDS STAINED BY THE BLOOD OF CYSTENNIN, THEY WERE ASTONISHED WHEN GWRTHEYRN RENEGED ON THEIR AGREEMENT.

ANGRY, THE VENGEFUL CYMRY TURNED AGAINST CYSTENNIN'S MURDERERS. THE PICTS HAD TO RUN AND FLEE WITHOUT BEING ABLE TO ACCOUNT FOR THEIR ACTIONS.

BUT THE PICTS WERE INCENSED AT GWRTHEYRN'S TREACHERY. THEY RAISED AN ARMY AND DESCENDED ON BRYTHON LANDS WITH FRENZIED DESTRUCTION.

NOW, AS HIGH KING, GWRTHEYRN MARCHED THE BRYTHON ARMY TO VICTORY, DECIMATING THE SAXON FORCE.

NEWS OF THE PICTISH THREAT TO TAKE HIS LIFE CAST FEAR INTO THE HEART OF GWRTHEYRN.

HE COULD NOT CALL ON THE BRYTHON CHIEFTAINS FOR AID WITHOUT DISCLOSING THE REASON FOR THE PICTISH FURY. IN HIS TERROR GWRTHEYRN MADE A FATAL DECISION, BEYOND ALL COMPREHENSION.

GWRTHEYRN TURNED TO HIS ARCH-ENEMIES, THE SAXONS, PROMISING LANDS IN BRITAIN SHOULD THEY STAND BESIDE HIM TO REPULSE THE PICTS.

WITHOUT DELAY THE SAXONS ACCEPTED GWRTHEYRN'S TREACHEROUS OFFER – AND WITH THE PICTS DEFEATED IN A BLOODY BATTLE, THE SAXONS CAME TO CLAIM THEIR PRIZE.

IT WAS GWRTHEYRN'S DECISION ALONE TO GIVE **HENGEST**, THE SAXON LEADER, AS MUCH LAND AS HE COULD ENCIRCLE WITH A SINGLE LEATHER TWINE.

AS CUNNING IN THOUGHT AS HE WAS MIGHTY IN BATTLE, HENGEST COMMANDED THAT A SINGLE LONG SINEW BE CUT FROM A BULL'S HIDE.

HIS INTENTION WAS TO SURROUND A MIGHTY OUTCROP WITH THIS LEATHER TWINE, AND THERE HE WOULD BUILD AN IMPREGNABLE FORTRESS.

THIS IS HOW SHAME AND CALUMNY BEFELL GWRTHEYRN. FROM BALAWON HEAD IN THE NORTH TO THE SOUTHERNMOST PROMONTORY OF PENWEDD IN CERNYW, GWRTHEYRN WAS MOST VILIFIED FOR HIS TREACHERY AMONGST HIS NATION, AND VISITED UPON HIMSELF HIS OWN DESTRUCTION.

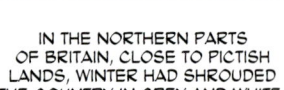

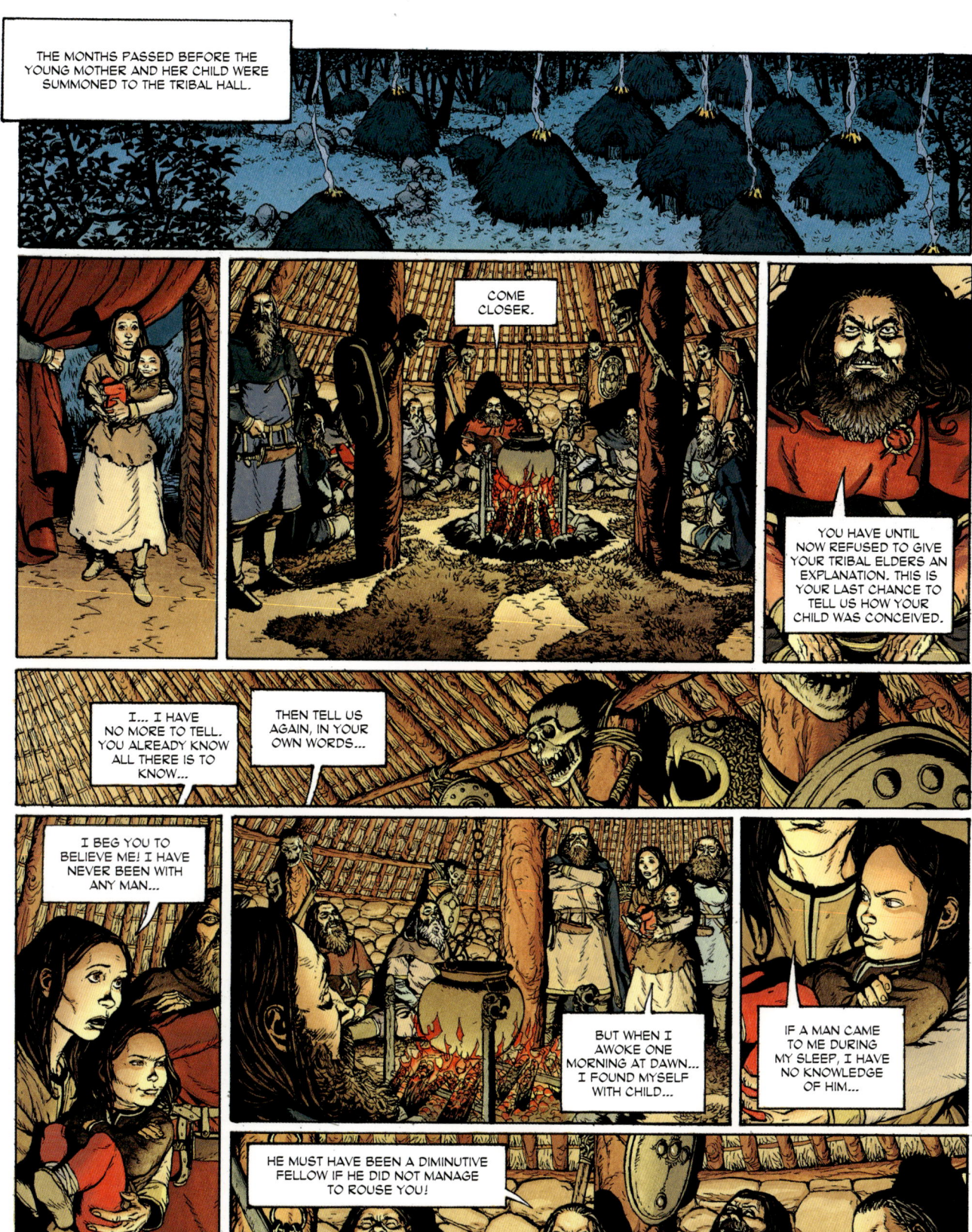

With the Brython princes in fine humour, Hengest rose to greet his guests.

He uttered three deadly words in his own reviled tongue, a secret message understood only by his men...
Draw your swords.

The Saxons drew the knives they had hidden in their shoes, plunging their blades into Brython throats.

This vile deed stained the ground blood red. Only two of the Brythons escaped alive.

The first was Gwrtheyrn. Hengest had decided to spare his life for ransom. The second was Eidol, prince of Caerloyw. Amid this horrid feast he managed to disarm his murdering adversary, and claimed a sharpened stake which he wielded to extinguish the lives of scores of his enemies.

Eidol recounted this **Treachery of the Long Knives** across the island, a salutary message of the Saxons' deception and scheming duplicity.

Throughout the whole of the Isle of the Mighty, the enraged Brythons seethed and gathered in preparation for war.

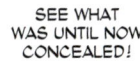

TWO DRAGONS ROSE FROM THE LAKE IN FURIOUS COMBAT, THEIR THUNDEROUS ROARS CARRYING TO THE FURTHEST PARTS OF BRITAIN.

THEIR WINGS BEAT THE AIR AS A CATACLYSMIC TEMPEST UNSEATING ROCKS, DEMOLISHING TREES AND SENDING HEDGEROWS FLYING IN ALL DIRECTIONS.

MERE MORTALS SCURRIED TO AND FRO, SEEKING REFUGE FROM THE FEROCIOUS UPROAR OF THE DRAGONS IN COMBAT ABOVE...

...BUT THEIR EFFORTS WERE IN VAIN. MILK IN THE BREASTS OF NURSING MOTHERS TURNED SOUR, THEIR CHILDREN FELL HELPLESS TO THE GROUND. LIVESTOCK SCURRIED MADLY, FOAMING AT THE MOUTH, EYES TURNED WHITE IN THEIR HEADS.

AS A GLARING BEACON, THE DRAGONS DUELLED ALL NIGHT LONG.

SHORTLY BEFORE DAWN, THE EXHAUSTED COHORT REACHED THE REGION OF CAER Y GARRAI.

THERE, UNDER THE DAWN'S EARLY LIGHT, THEY STOOD ASTOUNDED.

FOR THERE WERE THE STONES, ERECT IN A PERFECT RING, WHERE ON THE MIDSUMMER DAY OF ALBAN HEFIN THE SUN'S RAYS WOULD STRIKE THEM AND ILLUMINATE THE LAND ALL AROUND.

AND THERE TOO WAS MYRDDIN, RELAXING BENEATH THE STONES, CHEWING A STALK AS HE GLIMPSED THROUGH HALF-CLOSED EYES THE APPROACHING MULTITUDE.

ASTOUNDED IN THEIR MIDST WAS EMRYS AND HIS RETINUE.

THAT MORNING THE BRYTHONS, FILLED WITH PRIDE AT THE SIGHT OF THE MAGNIFICENT CONSTRUCTION, LAUDED MYRDDIN FOR HIS MISCHIEF.

WHEN ASKED HOW HE HAD ACHIEVED SUCH A FEAT, A SLIGHT KNOWING SMILE WOULD BE HIS ONLY ANSWER, LEAVING ALL NONE THE WISER.

IN THE MIDST OF THAT NIGHT'S FEASTING AND MERRIMENT, MYRDDIN AGAIN DISAPPEARED. THE KING ALONE KNEW OF HIS DESIRE TO DEPART, AND HAD CONSENTED TO HIS ABSENCE.

WITH BRITAIN SAFELY PROTECTED FROM WAR, EMRYS RETURNED TO HIS COURT AND DUTIES AS RULER OF HIS PEOPLE. MYRDDIN HEADED HOME TO THE VILLAGE WHERE HE WAS BORN.

THOSE YEARS OF ABSENCE HAD SEEN MYRDDIN GROW AND MATURE. HIS SISTER, GWENDDYDD, HAD ALSO BLOSSOMED INTO A DELIGHTFUL YOUNG WOMAN.

THE PREVIOUS SPRING, SHE HAD MARRIED A NEIGHBOURING CHIEFTAIN, **RHYDDERCH HAEL.**

TO HER ASTONISHMENT THAT SUMMER'S MORNING, HER BROTHER APPEARED. THEIR EYES HAD NOT MET FOR MANY YEARS, NOT SINCE HE'D RETURNED TO PAY HOMAGE AT THEIR MOTHER'S DEATHBED.

THAT DAY, THE FAMILY EMBRACED MYRDDIN. ALL WERE OVERJOYED AT BEING CLOSE TO KING EMRYS'S SOLE ADVISER, HE WHO WAS NOW LAUDED THROUGHOUT THE ISLE OF THE MIGHTY.

FOR THREE DAYS AND THREE NIGHTS THE FEASTING CONTINUED AT THE COURT OF RHYDDERCH HAEL, WITH FOOD AND DRINK APLENTY. AT THE FEAST WAS RHYDDERCH'S SISTER, **GWENDDOLEN.**

ALTHOUGH BEAUTIFUL AND STRONG-WILLED, SHE FELL AT ONCE UNDER MYRDDIN'S SPELL. HE ALSO NOTICED HER CHARMS, BLUSHING WHENEVER SHE CAME CLOSE.

BEFORE LONG, THEY BOTH EXPRESSED THEIR LOVE FOR EACH OTHER, AND WERE SOON JOINED IN MATRIMONY. MEN AND WOMEN FROM NEAR AND FAR CAME TO SHARE IN A BANQUET IN THEIR HONOUR.

MYRDDIN AND GWENDDOLEN SET UP HOME AT A FARMSTEAD CLOSE TO RHYDDERCH'S HOUSEHOLD, SPENDING LONG AND HAPPY HOURS TOGETHER. WHEN HER HUSBAND WOULD DEPART FOR DAYS, HIS YOUNG WIFE WOULD HAVE NO CARE IN THE WORLD.

IT WAS THERE AT ELFFIN'S HOME THAT I SPENT THE NEXT FOUR YEARS. DURING THAT TIME I GREW FROM A BOY TO THE YOUNG MAN YOU SEE BEFORE YOU TODAY, AND IN DOING SO FURTHER ASTONISHED GWYDDNO AND HIS FAMILY.

WHEN THERE I DID MY BEST TO CHEER MY BENEFACTOR ELFFIN. HE GRADUALLY CHANGED FROM A SHY YOUNG MAN WITH NO CONFIDENCE TO A MOST WITTY AND SOCIABLE INDIVIDUAL.

ONE AUTUMN DAY, ELFFIN DEPARTED ON A JOURNEY TO THE COURT AT DEGANWY, THERE INVITED BY HIS UNCLE, KING MAELGWN GWYNEDD.

AT DEGANWY, ELFFIN HAD HIS FILL OF FOOD AND DRINK, LISTENING TO THE BARDS SINGING KING MAELGWN'S PRAISES. BUT INEBRIATED, ELFFIN BEGAN BOASTING THAT HE, RATHER THAN MAELGWN, HAD THE MOST GIFTED BARD AND THE MOST FAITHFUL WIFE ANYWHERE IN THE WHOLE OF THE ISLAND OF BRITAIN.

BUT MAELGWN WAS A VICIOUS ADVERSARY. FURIOUS, HE CAST ELFFIN IN SHACKLES. HE THEN COMMANDED HIS BASTARD SON, RHUN — A HANDSOME YOUNG MAN WHO WOULD ENCHANT EVERY YOUNG GIRL WHO CAST EYES ON HIM — TO ENSNARE ELFFIN'S WIFE.

UPON LEARNING OF THIS CONSPIRACY, I AT ONCE WARNED MY PATRON'S WIFE, WHOM I PERSUADED TO DRESS HER MAID IN HER MISTRESS'S CLOTHES AND FINERY, AND FOR THIS MAID TO TAKE HER PLACE IN BED.

SO RHUN ONLY BEDDED THE MAID. BEFORE MORNING HE CUT OFF HER FINGER, WHICH CARRIED ELFFIN'S RING, THEN SWIFTLY RETURNED TO DEGANWY.

AT DEGANWY, ELFFIN WAS DRAGGED FROM HIS CELL TO BE SHOWN PROOF OF HIS WIFE'S INFIDELITY.

A FINGER TOO SMALL AND A NAIL TOO DIRTY! SEE HOW THE SKIN IS COARSE. THIS IS NOT MY WIFE'S FINGER!

ANGERED AGAIN, MAELGWN CAST ELFFIN BACK IN CHAINS. I WAS WITNESS TO IT ALL, BECAUSE, UNBEKNOWN TO RHUN, I HAD FOLLOWED HIM BACK TO COURT AS HE SPED HOME.

LATER THAT NIGHT, AS THE CHIEF BARD HEININ ENTERTAINED THE RETINUE, THREE COURT POETS BEGAN RECOUNTING TALES OF MAELGWN'S MAJESTY.

With Emrys's force following on behind, Myrddin raced northward like the blowing wind, to the camp of King Gwynddolau.

GWYNDDOLAU!

I am Myrddin, counsellor to King Emrys! I am tasked to put an end to the madness that has gripped you!

I know who you are. Give me your message – I am hungry, and my patience is short when my stomach grumbles for food!

Your wisdom is feeble, Gwynddolau!...

...and lacking wisdom you will be answerable for spilling the blood of the Cymry and defiling our nation's new-found peace.

Desist from turning friend against friend, brother against brother and father against son!

Heed my words before punishment befalls you and your name be cursed throughout the Island of Britain!

Come and find me on the hill at dawn with your answer.

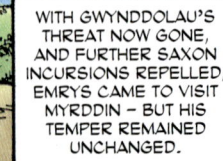

THE SEASONS PASSED WITHOUT CHANGE FOR MYRDDIN'S TORTURE. AT TIMES HE WAS SEEN IN CONVERSATION WITH THE TREES AND BEASTS, OR EVEN BRAYING COUNTLESS CURSES TOWARDS THE SKY FOR THE INSANITY THAT POSSESSED HIM.

IN DEFENCE OF A NEIGHBOURING FRIENDLY CLAN DURING A CONFLICT WITH OTHER TRIBES, RHYDDERCH LOST HIS LIFE.

RATHER THAN ASSUME HER HUSBAND'S ROLE AS LEADER OF HER TRIBE, GWENDDYDD, IN HER SORROW, JOINED HER BROTHER IN THE HEART OF THE FOREST. THERE SHE MADE FOR THEM A HOME, SHELTER AGAINST THE WINTER'S BITE.

THERE, ALONE, SHE CARED DAY AND NIGHT FOR THE ONE SHE WOULD OFTEN CALL HER LITTLE BROTHER.

SOMETIMES, WHEN BRIEFLY RELEASED FROM HIS INSANITY, MYRDDIN WOULD REVEAL THE POWERS OF PLANTS AND TREES TO HIS SISTER, AND TEACH HER THE LANGUAGE OF THE FOREST ANIMALS.

BUT WHEN HIS HORROR RETURNED HE WOULD CURL UP AND CRY LIKE A CHILD, HIS EYES BULGING WITH FEAR. AT HAND, ONLY GWENDDYDD, THERE TO COMFORT HIM WITH HER SWEET VOICE AND TENDERNESS.

SUCH WAS HIS CONDITION ONE AUTUMN DAY WHEN TALIESIN CAME UPON HIM, HAVING JOURNEYED OVER DISTANT LANDS SEEKING HIS DEAR FRIEND.

REALIZING HIS STATE, TALIESIN VOWED NOT TO REST UNTIL HE FOUND A CURE FOR MYRDDIN, EVEN IF THAT MEANT SEARCHING UNTIL HIS DYING DAY.

ONE MORNING, WITH SUMMER AND AUTUMN LONG PAST AND TALIESIN'S VISIT A DISTANT MEMORY, GWENDDYDD AWOKE FROM HER SLEEP OF FIVE DREAMS.

SHE ASKED HER BROTHER TO EXPLAIN THE DREAMS THAT HAD DISTURBED HER SLUMBER.

I SAW A PLAIN COVERED WITH CAIRNS, BOTH LARGE AND SMALL, WITH MEN CARRYING STONES TO AND FRO, FROM THE SMALL MOUNDS TO THE LARGER PILES.

THESE CAIRNS ARE THE PEOPLE OF BRITAIN, NOBLES AND PEASANTS.

THE MEN YOU SAW WERE THE NOBLES' SERVANTS, DISINHERITING THE PEASANTS TO FURTHER ENRICH THEIR MASTERS.

I SAW STRONG ALDER TREES CUT DOWN BY ARROGANT MEN CLEAVING WITH RAZORED AXES. BUT FROM THE TREES GREW EVEN STRONGER ALDERS.

THE ALDERS ARE THE PRIDE OF BRITAIN'S PEOPLE. THE ARROGANT MEN ARE THE FOREIGN INVADERS, OUR FOES, WHO ADVANCE TO BREAK US IN INTERMINABLE CONFLICT.

BUT DESPITE THE RUIN, BETTER AND STRONGER MEN WILL FOLLOW.

I SAW THE LAND DAPPLED WITH ROLLING HILLS. EACH ONE DISAPPEARED AND WAS REPLACED BY ENORMOUS FOUL DUNG HEAPS. BUT SOON, MAGNIFICENT FLOWERS BEGAN TO GERMINATE IN THE PILES.

THE LAND IS BRITAIN, THE HILLS OUR OLD CHIEFTAINS. THE DUNG HEAPS ARE OUR VAIN NEW LEADERS, BROTHERLY TOWARDS THE INVADER.

THE FLOWERS ARE OUR FUTURE LEADERS, THOSE WHO WILL RESTORE THIS ISLAND TO ITS PAST GLORY.

I SAW A FIELD OF GOLDEN WHEAT. THEN A HERD OF SWINE CAME AND DEVOURED THE WHEAT, BEFORE BEING DRIVEN AWAY BY A PACK OF VICIOUS HOUNDS.

THE FIELD IS THE ISLAND OF BRITAIN.

THE SWINE ARE OUR ENEMIES, DESTROYING OUR LAND. THE DOGS ARE THE BRYTHON WARRIORS WHO WILL DRIVE THEM AWAY.

I SAW A VAST GRAVEYARD WHERE SCORES OF WOMEN LAY, HEAVY WITH THEIR UNBORN CHILDREN, EACH CHILD TALKING TO THE OTHER FROM HIS MOTHER'S WOMB.

THE GRAVEYARD IS THE ISLAND OF BRITAIN. THE WOMEN ARE A SIGN THAT THIS ISLAND'S YOUTH WILL GO FORTH AND POPULATE OUR LAND.

THEIR CHILDREN WILL BE EVEN WISER THAN THOSE WHO HAVE ALREADY WALKED THIS EARTH.

DURING THIS TIME, SUCCESS HAD ELUDED TALIESIN.

THE YOUTHFUL BARD HAD SCOURED THE LENGTH AND BREADTH OF BRITAIN, IRELAND AND BRITTANY.

WHEREVER HE WENT HE WOULD CONVERSE WITH WISE MEN AND OLD WOMEN, THEIR FACES CREASED WITH AGE, ASKING WHAT WOULD RELEASE MYRDDIN FROM HIS TRIAL. BUT NOBODY KNEW.

FATIGUED AND IN DESPAIR, TALIESIN DROWSED AT THE FOOT OF A CHESTNUT TREE

WHEN HE AWOKE, HIS EYES WERE CAST ON A LAND HE HAD NOT BEHELD BEFORE.

A LAND OF GENTLE BREEZE, OF AIR SO SWEET, THE BLUE SKY ABOVE MORE BRILLIANT THAN THE AZURE SEA.

ABOUT HIM WERE GIGANTIC APPLE TREES, THEIR BRANCHES HEAVY WITH THE MOST LUSCIOUS FRUIT.

NEARBY SPRUNG FORTH A SOURCE OF CLEAR BRIGHT WATER. IN AN INSTANT TALIESIN KNEW HIS QUEST WAS AT AN END.

HIS HANDS REACHED FOR HIS HARP, HIS FINGERS GENTLY PULLING AT THE STRINGS. HE BEGAN SINGING AND WALKING, BECKONING THE WATER TO FOLLOW.

FOR COUNTLESS DAYS AND NIGHTS HE LED THE WATER ALONG ITS COURSE, WITHOUT ONCE PAUSING HIS SONG IN VOICE OR MUSIC.

UNTIL ONE EXHAUSTED EVENING HE ARRIVED AT THE HOME OF MYRDDIN AND GWENDDYDD AMONGST THE TREES.

WHEN SHE SAW THIS WONDROUS MYSTERY, GWENDDYDD KNEW AT ONCE THAT TALIESIN HAD KEPT HIS WORD, AND SHE LED MYRDDIN TOWARDS THE SPRING WATER.

MYRDDIN CUPPED HIS HANDS TO RAISE THE LIVING WATER TO HIS LIPS. AT ONCE HIS CLOAK OF MADNESS WAS TORN AWAY AS SANITY AND SENSE RETURNED TO HIM.

HE BEGAN TO TREMBLE AS TEARS WELLED IN HIS HEART. FOR A MOMENT HIS SISTER THOUGHT HE HAD BEEN POISONED.

CURED... I'M CURED!

ON HEARING HIS FRIEND UTTER THESE WORDS, AND DRAINED OF ALL HIS STRENGTH, TALIESIN LET GO HIS HARP AND HIS SONG ENDED.

HE FELL AT THE FEET OF MYRDDIN AND GWENDDYDD AS THE GLISTENING WATER RETURNED DEEP INTO THE GROUND, WITHOUT LEAVING A SINGLE DROP BEHIND.

TALIESIN WAS TAKEN INTO THE DWELLING, THEN MYRDDIN LEFT HIM WITH GWENDDYDD AS HE WENT INTO THE FOREST IN SEARCH OF PLANTS AND ROOTS TO REVIVE HIS FAITHFUL FRIEND.

TALIESIN SLEPT FOR THREE DAYS AND NIGHTS. MYRDDIN AND GWENDDYDD THOUGHT HIM DEAD – BUT THEN THE BARD OPENED HIS EYES AND GAZED AT MYRDDIN, WHO SHED GENTLE TEARS OF JOY.

SLEEP AGAIN, TALIESIN. YOU RESCUED ME, NOW YOU MUST REST.

WHEN YOU GROW STRONG AGAIN WE SHALL TALK AND BE ON OUR WAY. MY TRIBULATIONS WERE LONG, AND THE ISLE OF THE MIGHTY IS IN DESPERATE NEED OF US BOTH.

SOMETHING GREAT HAS COME TO PASS. WE HAVE BEEN GIVEN A LEADER, FAR MIGHTIER THAN ANY OTHER EVER WITNESSED IN OUR LAND. HE WILL NEED COURAGEOUS MEN TO STAND WITH HIM IN DEFENDING BRITAIN.

END OF THE FIRST BOOK

ARTHUR THE LEGEND

BOOK 2

ARTHUR

PROTECTOR OF BRITAIN

People & Places

LLOEGR is the modern-day Welsh name for England but also attested in early sources, and often linked to the Anglo-Saxon kingdom of Mercia.

CAI HIR, Cai 'the Long', son of Cynyr Cainfarfog (Fairbeard) in the native Welsh Arthurian tale of *Culhwch and Olwen*. One of Arthur's most constant companions. Brother of **GWYAR**, and foster-brother to Arthur and his sisters **MORGEN** and **ANNA**, whose blood-parents were Uthr Pendragon and Eurgain of **GELLI WIG** in **CERNYW** (Cornwall).

BEDWYR BEDRYDANT – or Bedwyr of the Perfect Sinews – is one of Arthur's earliest companions in the Welsh Arthurian tradition, his name associated with Arthur in legends and poetry.

CAERLLION AR WYSG is the old Roman legionary fortress of Isca Silurum on the banks of the river Wysg (Usk) in south-east Wales, its remarkable remains long-associated with Arthur. In the Welsh Triads poems, Caerllion is described as the location of one of Arthur's three courts.

GWION LLYGAD CATH (Gwion Cat's Eye) along with **CYNDDYLIG GYFARWYDD**, **LLENLLEOG** and Arthur's other companions in his ever-increasing warband, are all mentioned as Arthur's men in the native Welsh Arthurian legend *Culhwch and Olwen*.

CAER SIDDI is an alternative name for the Celtic otherworld of Annwfn. The early Welsh poem *Spoils of Annwfn* mentions Arthur sailing to Caer Siddi in his ship **PRYDWEN**. The tale is echoed in *Culhwch and Olwen*, where Arthur appropriates a magic cauldron and his sword **CALEDFWLCH** at the court of **DIWRNACH**.

MODRON is the Welsh form of the Celtic mother-goddess *Matrona*, whose son **MABON** was stolen from her when he was three nights old.

MÔN, the Mother Isle, is the island of Anglesey, which contained three ancient territorial divisions called 'cantrefi' or 'hundreds'.

BENDIGEIDFRAN, or Brân the Blessed, is central to the tale of his sister **BRANWEN** in the collection of legends called the *Mabinogi*. As King of Britain he ventures to avenge Branwen's mistreatment at the hand of king **MATHOLWCH** in Ireland, news of which Bendigeidfran received at his court in **CAER SAINT YN ARFON** (or Caernarfon) located at the Roman fort of Segontium. During his foray to Ireland he crosses the mystical river **LLINON** (Shannon) before being mortally wounded. Bendigeidfran commands that his head should be taken to the isle of **GWALES** in Penfro (the island of Grassholm in Pembroke), overlooking **ABER HENFELEN**, the sea between Wales and Cernyw and **DYFNAINT** (Devon), before being taken to be buried at the **GWYNFRYN**, the White Hill – possibly Tower Hill – in London.

HYWEL SON OF EMRYS LLYDAW is one of Arthur's main companions. According to Geoffrey of Monmouth's *Historia Regum Britanniae*, Hywel was Arthur's nephew.

LLUMONWY is one of the lakes mentioned in the *Historia Brittonum* as being among the Wonders of Britain. Located in modern Scotland, this is Loch Lomond. The other lakes mentioned, the **FOUNT OF GORHELI** and lake **LLIWAN** by the estuary of the river **HAFREN** (Severn), remain to be identified.

MOUNT BADDON is the twelfth of Arthur's battles according to the *Historia Brittonum*. The *Annales Cambriae* gives the battle's date as 516, while Gildas assigns Emrys Wledig as the battle's victor. It follows Arthur's first campaign at the mouth of the river Glein; the next four battles by the river Dulas; the sixth battle at the river Bassas; the seventh is the battle at the Forest of Celyddon; the eighth close to Gwynnion fort; the ninth at the City of the Legion; the tenth on the bank of the river Tryfrwyd; the eleventh on the hill called Agned; and the twelfth on Baddon hill where Arthur alone killed 960 men and was victorious.

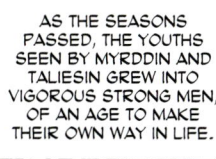

AS THE SEASONS PASSED, THE YOUTHS SEEN BY MYRDDIN AND TALIESIN GREW INTO VIGOROUS STRONG MEN, OF AN AGE TO MAKE THEIR OWN WAY IN LIFE.

AS PROPHESIED BY MYRDDIN, CAI MATURED INTO A TALL YOUNG MAN. BUT IT WAS ARTHUR, SHORTER AND STOCKIER, WHO WOULD PESTER CYNYR TO BE ALLOWED TO LEAVE HIS COURT IN SEARCH OF GLORY.

MORGEN WAS AS BEAUTIFUL AS EVER, BUT STILL KEPT HER OWN COMPANY AS SHE DID WHEN A CHILD.

ANNA AND GWYAR GREW CLOSE, IN ATTRACTION AND AFFECTION. EVENTUALLY THEY FELL IN LOVE.

AND FROM THIS LOVE A CHILD WAS BORN TO THEM DEEP IN THE FOREST, AWAY FROM FAMILY AND RELATIONS, SO AS NOT TO INCUR WRATH AT AN ILLEGITIMATE BIRTH.

TO AVOID DISGRACE THE YOUNG LOVERS HAD NO CHOICE BUT TO HAND THE BABY INTO THE CARE OF A PASSING WARRIOR. HAVING PONDERED OVER THEIR DILEMMA, THE STRANGER AGREED TO TAKE THE CHILD.

HIS ONE CONDITION WAS THAT HE WOULD RAISE THE CHILD AS HIS OWN. TURNING THEIR BACKS ON THE BABE IN ARMS, THE YOUNG COUPLE WERE STRUCK BY GRIEF AND THEIR SOULS DESCENDED INTO A DARKENED ABYSS.

THE WARRIOR SWIFTLY DEPARTED. BUT UNBEKNOWN TO HIM A WONDROUS FUTURE WAS AHEAD OF THE NEWBORN CHILD, A CHILD WEARING A PENDANT THAT WOULD BEAR WITNESS TO HIS INHERITANCE.

CYNYR HAD BEEN AWARE FOR SOME TIME THAT CAI'S AND ARTHUR'S ENTHUSIASM FOR FIGHTING WOULD SURPASS HIS OWN DESIRES TO KEEP THEM SAFE AT HOME.

IT WAS A SAD DAY WHEN HIS TWO SONS DEPARTED IN SEARCH OF GLORY. OF ALL THEIR KIN, ONLY CYNYR KNEW THE TWO YOUNG MEN WERE ABOUT TO LEAVE.

IN EMBRACING BOTH, CYNYR GREATLY DESIRED THAT ARTHUR SHOULD SHOW CAI HOW TO PERFORM ON THE BATTLEFIELD.

BUT WISELY, HE KNEW TO KEEP HIS CONCERNS TO HIMSELF AND NOT TO SMOTHER HIS SONS WITH HIS OWN DOUBTS AT THIS MOMENTOUS TIME.

AT THE END OF THE DAY, AS THE SUN SLOWLY FELL BEHIND THE HORIZON, THE YOUNG MEN BEGAN TO FEEL WEARY...

CAI?

WHAT?!

LISTEN! DO YOU HEAR THAT?

NO...

THAT'S HOW WE WILL BE ONE DAY — THE GROUND WILL SHUDDER BENEATH THE THUNDEROUS HOOVES OF OUR HORSES!

MAYBE SO!... BUT FOR NOW, LET'S FIND SOMETHING TO EAT, BEFORE WE STARVE!

"What about it?"

"I don't know... Arthur, what do you think?!"

"I say we should wait till midnight, garrotte the guards and take all the horses."

"Even if we lose some of the animals during our escape, it will stop them from following us."

"I disagree. If we kill the guards, we'll be hunted down come what may."

"It's far less risky to take just three horses."

"Bedwyr... what do you say?"

"I've yet to hear anything that makes sense."

"Tell me, Myrddin... what news from Caerllion ar Wysg?"

"Is King Emrys well?"

"He is... but still without heir."

"Did he not take a new wife?"

"He did, but their love has not yet borne fruit..."

...HEADING TOWARDS CYNYR'S VILLAGE.

DESPITE HIS LONG ABSENCE, MYRDDIN RECEIVED A WARM WELCOME.

CYNYR WAS CONCERNED FOR HIS SONS, HIS THOUGHTS EVIDENT TO MYRDDIN.

CAI AND ARTHUR ARE WELL, CYNYR. BOTH WILL SOON ATTAIN THE GLORY THEY HAVE SO LONG DESIRED.

MYRDDIN'S WORDS GAVE CYNYR GREAT COMFORT. IN HIS GRATITUDE HE INVITED THE SEER TO STAY AS HIS GUEST FOR AS LONG AS HE WISHED.

GOOD DAY, MORGEN, SPRINGTIME'S BRILLIANT BLOOM.

GOOD DAY, MYRDDIN.

WHY DO YOU SEEK ME, FAIR MAIDEN? NOT BECAUSE OF MY SECRET AGE NOR THE MYSTERIOUS SIGNS THAT SURROUND ME, I'LL WAGER.

IT IS SAID YOU ARE A FAMED SORCERER AND SOOTHSAYER.

TRUE... PERHAPS...

AND WHAT IF I WERE TO SAY YOU ARE A DECEIVER OF MEN?

ARTHUR WAS FIRST TO STRIKE.

AS THE BATTLE RAGED, THE SURROUNDING VALLEY WAS DEAFENED BY THE STRAINING OF HORSES, THE AGONIZED CRIES OF WOUNDED WARRIORS AND BY IRON STRIKING SHIELDS AND SHATTERED BONE.

THE BATTLE'S FORTUNES SWUNG BETWEEN THE ADVERSARIES, THEN...

WITH THEIR WARLORD DEAD, THE CYMRY SCATTERED AS THEY LOST ALL DIRECTION...

THIS SINGLE ACT ENCOURAGED THE BRYTHONS ANEW. THE BATTLE TURNED IN THEIR FAVOUR, AND FINALLY VICTORY WAS THEIRS.

THE VICTORIOUS BAND CONGREGATED TO PLEDGE ALLEGIANCE TO ARTHUR. DESPITE A BLOODIED FOREHEAD, HE WAS GREATLY PLEASED.

AS WAS CUSTOMARY, THE LAST WARRIOR TO ENGAGE IN BATTLE OFFERED HIS LIFE TO HIS LEADER. BUT ARTHUR REFUSED TO TAKE ANY FURTHER BRYTHON SACRIFICE.

ARTHUR'S REPUTE WAS MADE GREATER BY HIS GESTURE. HE WAS ELECTED THE WARBAND'S NEW LEADER AND HIS FRIENDS CAI AND BEDWYR SWELLED WITH PRIDE.

FROM THAT DAY, ARTHUR ASSUMED HIS PREDECESSOR'S MANTLE. HE LED HIS WARRIORS TO PILLAGE AND PLUNDER ENEMY TERRITORY, GAINING VICTORY TIME AFTER TIME.

HE WOULD CARRY THE SPOILS TO BRYTHON VILLAGES AND DIVIDE THEM AMONG THE CYMRY – OR EQUALLY BETWEEN HIS MEN. BEFORE LONG, HIS NAME WAS RENOWNED ALONG THE FRONTIER AND FAR BEYOND.

MANY WARRIORS JOINED HIS CAUSE, FIGHTING FOR JUSTICE, RICHES AND GLORY. SOON HIS WARBAND HAD GROWN INTO A SMALL ARMY.

IN THE VANGUARD, **GWION LLYGAD CATH**, WHOSE EYESIGHT WAS SO KEEN THAT HE COULD REMOVE A SPECK FROM A GNAT'S EYE... WITHOUT HARMING THE EYE.

NEXT TO HIM RODE **CYNDDYLIG GYFARWYDD**, THE GUIDE WHO COULD SECURELY LEAD THE WARBAND THROUGH FAMILIAR AND STRANGE LANDS WHEREVER THEY WERE.

THEN THERE WAS **MORFRAN**, SON OF TEGID FOEL AND CERIDWEN. DESPITE HIS UNRIVALLED DEFORMITY, HE HAD LEFT HIS FAMILY IN SEARCH OF FAME AND ADVENTURE.

NEXT TO HIM, THE YOUNG RAPTUROUS GAELIC WARRIOR **LLENLLEOG**.

NEXT CAME **HENBEDDESTYR SON OF ERIM** – THE STRIDER OF OLD – WHO COULD RUN AS FAST AS A HORSE COULD GALLOP.

BY HIS SIDE, **GLEWLWYD GAFAELFAWR**, WHOSE HANDS POSSESSED A MIGHTY GRASP. A WARRIOR OF IMPRESSIVE STATURE, HIS ARMS THICK AS TREE TRUNKS, HIS THIGHS STURDY AS BOULDERS.

ASTRIDE THE NEXT HORSE, THE WARRIOR **HENWAS EDEINIOG**, WHO WOULD NOT TURN HIS BACK ON THE FRAY BEFORE ANY INJURY HE HAD SUSTAINED PROVED NEAR FATAL.

THEN **HUAIL**, SON OF **CAW THE PICT**, KING OF **CWM CAWLWYD**. WHILE AWAITING HIS SUCCESSION, HUAIL HAD GONE IN SEARCH OF GLORY AND HONOUR.

THEN FOLLOWED A PROUD FORCE OF WARRIORS. AMONGST THEM **DREM SON OF DREMHIDYDD**, WHOSE SHARP EYES COULD SEE FROM GELLI WIG IN CERNYW TO BALAWON AT THE MOST NORTHERN POINT OF THE ISLAND; **HIR ATRWM** AND **HIR ERWM**, TWO BROTHERS WITH UNUSUALLY MIGHTY APPETITES...

...**SGILTI YSGAFNDROED**, WHOSE LIGHT FOOTSTEPS WOULD NOT EVEN BREAK A BLADE OF GRASS; **TEITHI HEN**, UPON WHOSE KNIFE A HAFT WOULD NEVER STAY; AND **HYGWYDD**, ARTHUR'S STEWARD, ALWAYS AT HIS LEADER'S SIDE.

ALL HELD ARTHUR IN HIGH ESTEEM, READY TO FOLLOW HIM FROM ONE END OF THE ISLAND TO THE OTHER AND PREPARED, IF NECESSARY, TO GIVE UP THEIR LIVES FOR HIM.

FINELY ROBED, EXQUISITELY ARMED, ARRAYED IN GLORIOUS BROOCHES AND SATISFIED WITH PROVISIONS, WHEREVER THE WARBAND WENT IT WAS ALWAYS VICTORIOUS AND HIGHLY PRAISED.

BEFORE LONG, ARTHUR AND HIS COMPANIONS REACHED THE SKERRY.

THERE THEY WERE WELCOMED BY **DIWRNACH**, COUNSEL TO **ODGAR SON OF AEDD**, HIGH KING OF IRELAND.

THEY WERE ESCORTED TO DIWRNACH'S COURT, NESTLING BENEATH THE BROCH – SUCH A TOWER AS NEVER BEFORE SEEN BY ARTHUR AND HIS RETINUE.

DIWRNACH EXTENDED A WARM WELCOME TO HIS GUESTS, BUT HIS KIND WORDS CONCEALED A DEEP MISTRUST OF HIS VISITORS.

HE LONGED TO KNOW WHY ARTHUR HAD VENTURED ACROSS THE SEA – THIS VALIANT WARRIOR ARTHUR WHO NOW STOOD DISHEVELLED IN HIS HALL.

FACE TO FACE, ARTHUR AND DIWRNACH PRAISED EACH OTHER WITH COURTLY ETIQUETTE AND FLATTERY.

SUCH INDULGENCE WAS CUSTOMARY, AND ARTHUR WAS RECEIVED WITH THE SAME FORMALITY AS HE HIMSELF WOULD HAVE EXTENDED.

IN THE PASSAGE TO THE GREAT HALL, HE MET **MODRON**, MISTRESS OF THE CASTLE, AND WIFE TO DIWRNACH.

MUCH TO THE ASTONISHMENT OF ARTHUR AND HIS RETINUE, MODRON GREETED THEM ALL BY THEIR FIRST NAMES AND TOOK THEM TO FEAST WITH DIWRNACH AND HIS HOUSEHOLD.

AS THEY GLADLY ACCEPTED THE INVITATION TO THE BANQUET, DIWRNACH'S BARDS BEGAN SINGING THEIR CHIEFTAIN'S PRAISES AS THE HOUSEHOLD PREPARED THE HALL.

WITH ALL PRESENT IN GOOD HUMOUR, ARTHUR ASKED DIWRNACH ABOUT THE TWO MAGIC TREASURES HE POSSESSED.

THE FIRST WAS A CAULDRON UNRIVALLED ANYWHERE IN ALL THE LANDS. THE SECOND, AN EXQUISITE SWORD WITH SUCH A DAZZLING BLADE THAT NO MERE MORTAL COULD EVER WIELD IT.

AS ARTHUR POSED HIS QUESTION, DIWRNACH'S EYES OPENED WIDE. INDEED, HE REPLIED, HE DID POSSESS THE CAULDRON OF PLENTY – BUT THE SWORD WAS A FIGMENT OF IMAGINATION.

WITH THAT, THE WONDROUS CAULDRON WAS BROUGHT INTO THE HALL.

DIWRNACH'S CAULDRON SHIMMERED IN THE LIGHT, ITS INTRICATE DESIGN ELABORATE, MORE MAGNIFICENT AND STUNNING THAN ANY OTHER CAULDRON EVER SEEN.

THE CAULDRON BRIMMED WITH MAGIC, A VESSEL OF PLENTY THAT COULD PROVIDE SUSTENANCE TO SCORES OR HUNDREDS OR THOUSANDS OF WARRIORS.

ARTHUR AND HIS COMPANIONS WERE BLINDED AS THEY GAZED UPON THE SUMPTUOUS CAULDRON, DUMBFOUNDED IN ADMIRATION.

THEN DIWRNACH SPOTTED THE GLOWING DESIRE IN ARTHUR'S EYES, CONFIRMING HIS SUSPICIONS SURROUNDING THIS VISIT TO HIS SEABOUND CITADEL.

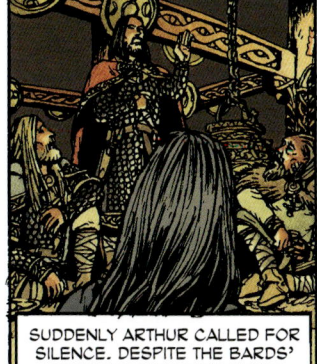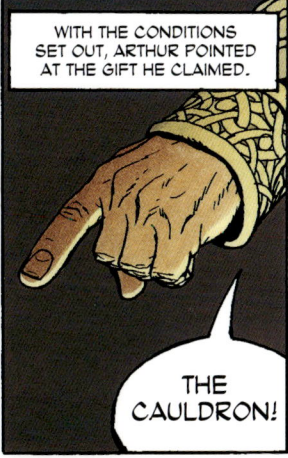

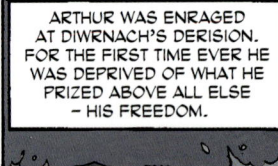

THE FOLLOWING MORNING ARTHUR LED HIS WARBAND TO BATTLE, A WARBAND THAT HAD NOW GROWN TO OVER A HUNDRED MEN.

A HORDE OF SAXONS HAD LANDED ON THE BRYTHON SHORES, AND WERE AGAIN ATTEMPTING TO CAPTURE CYMRY LANDS AND TO ANNEX NEW TERRITORIES.

BUT ARTHUR WAS ALWAYS THERE TO STAND FAST. THE ENEMY WAS ANNIHILATED WHEREVER HE WENT, THE GROUND BENEATH SODDEN WITH BLOOD.

OVER THREE UNTIRING SPRING SEASONS ARTHUR DARTED BACK AND FORTH ALONG THE BORDER, CHALLENGING THE SAXONS WHEREVER THEY OPPRESSED – BE THEY HIDDEN IN TREES, ON THE BANKS OF LAKES OR BOGGED DOWN ON MARSHY PLAINS.

WARRING FROM DAWN TILL DUSK AND AGAIN TILL DAWN, IN GOLDEN SUNSHINE AND SILVER MOONLIGHT, ARTHUR WOULD BE FOUND SWORD IN HAND.

WINTER OR SUMMER, RAIN OR SHINE, IN BLINDING BLIZZARDS OR STEELY GREY MISTS, THE BATTLES CONTINUED.

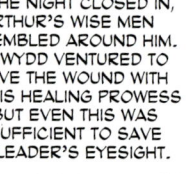

From one end of the island to the other, greater numbers came to join Arthur's warband, which by now resembled a mighty army.

Amongst the newly gathered warriors was **Gwrhyr Gwastod Ieithoedd**. He was fluent in all the languages of men and beasts. He was Arthur's interpreter.

With him was **Clust son of Clustfeiniad**, whose hearing was so sharp he could hear a tiny ant leave its nest over distant hundreds.

Behind them, **Gwaddyn Oddiaith**, whose feet would spark as he walked over stony ground...

...and with him, **Gwaddyn Osol**, whose bulk was so great he could flatten a high mountain into a level plain.

NEXT CAME GWEFYL SON OF GWASTAD WHOSE WONDROUS LIPS COULD STRETCH AND PROTECT A GROWN MAN.

HE WAS ACCOMPANIED BY OSLA GYLLELLFAWR, WHO OWNED THE MAGIC KNIFE BRONLLAFN FERLYDAN. WHEN LAIN ACROSS A RIVER, ITS BLADE WOULD REACH THE OTHER SIDE TO ALLOW ARTHUR'S ARMY TO CROSS THE TORRENT BENEATH.

THEN SUGN SON OF SUGNEDYDD, A MAN WITH A BLAZING FIRE IN HIS BELLY AND WHO COULD DRINK A RIVERBED DRY TO QUENCH HIS THIRST.

THERE FOLLOWED SOL, WHO COULD STAND ON ONE LEG FOR A WHOLE DAY.

BEHIND THESE MEN RODE EIRINWYCH AMHEIBYN, ARTHUR'S STEWARD IN HYGWYDD'S ABSENCE, GERAINT SON OF ERBIN, GWYN SON OF NUDD, BOTH WARRIORS OF NOTE, GWEIR SON OF GWEIRYDD AND MADOG SON OF TWRGADARN.

NEVER BEFORE DID A RETINUE HAVE SO MUCH FAITH IN ITS WARLEADER'S VICTORIOUS STRENGTH. IN TURN, ARTHUR WAS DAILY EMBOLDENED TO THE FRAY...

ATTACK!

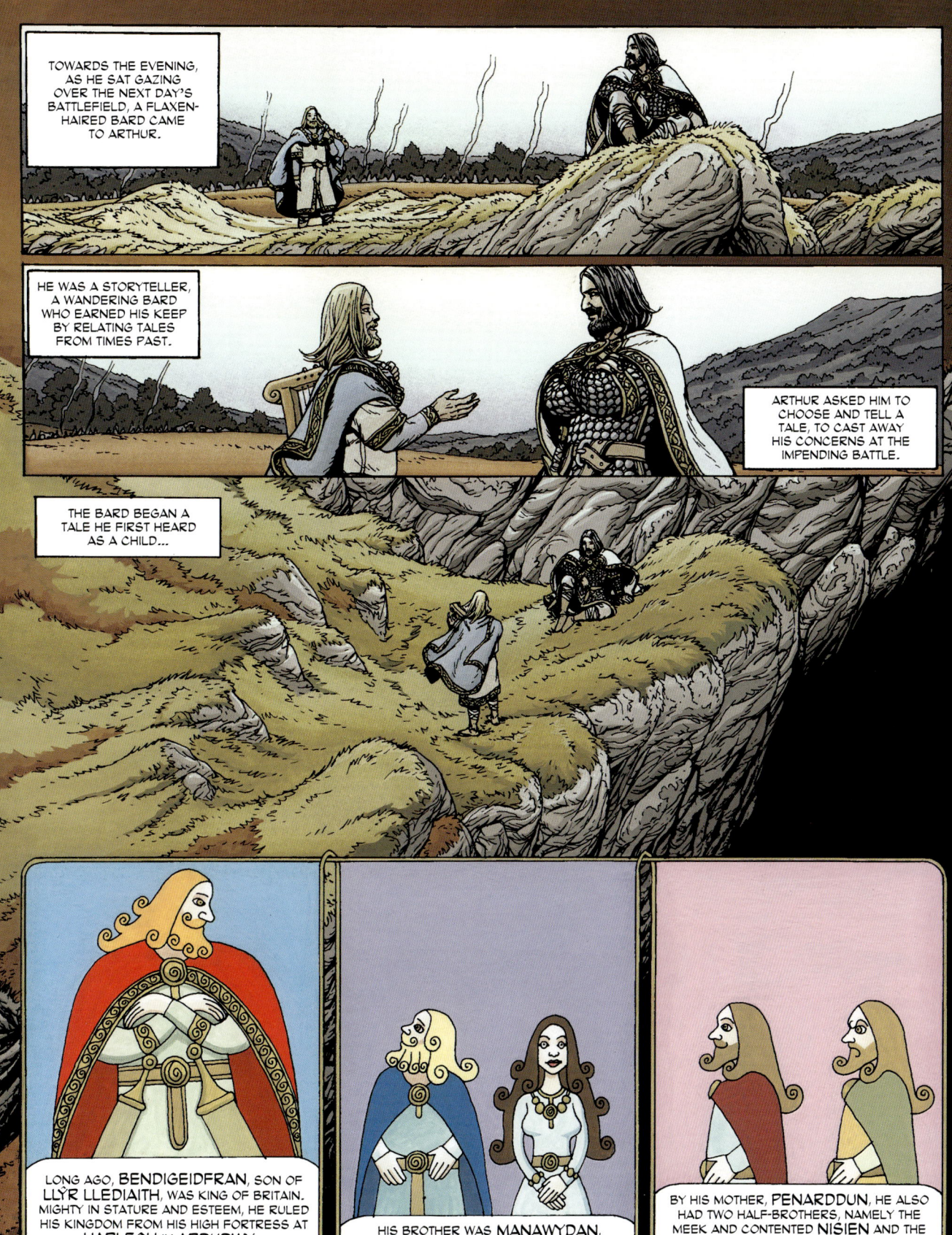

ONE DAY, SITTING ON A ROCK HIGH ABOVE THE WAVES, BENDIGEIDFRAN SAW THIRTEEN SHIPS SAILING HIS WAY FROM **IRELAND**.

HE COMMANDED HIS BROTHERS AND MEN TO WELCOME THESE VISITORS, WHOSE PEACEFUL INTENTIONS WERE DISPLAYED BY A SHIELD PLACED ATOP THE SAIL.

AT THE HEAD OF THIS DAZZLING FLEET WAS **MATHOLWCH**, HIGH KING OF IRELAND. HE TOLD BENDIGEIDFRAN HE HAD COME TO SEEK BRANWEN'S HAND IN MARRIAGE.

HAVING CONSIDERED AWHILE, BENDIGEIDFRAN AGREED TO MATHOLWCH'S REQUEST, THEIR ESPOUSAL TO TAKE PLACE AT **ABERFFRAW** ON THE MOTHER ISLE.

MATHOLWCH AND HIS FLEET SAILED FORTH TO ABERFFRAW, AS BENDIGEIDFRAN MARCHED THERE WITH HIS ENTOURAGE TO CELEBRATE THE UNION OF BRANWEN AND MATHOLWCH.

BENEATH AN ACRE OF PAVILIONS, AS NO SINGLE HALL WAS VAST ENOUGH TO ACCOMMODATE BENDIGEIDFRAN, A CONVIVIAL WEDDING FEAST OF MERRIMENT WAS HELD.

BUT EFNISIEN WAS NOT CONSULTED ON THE UNION. WHEN HE WAS TOLD OF THE BETROTHAL HE WAS FILLED WITH RAGE AND FELL UPON MATHOLWCH'S HORSES.

HE CUT THEIR LIPS BACK TO THEIR TEETH, THEIR EARS DOWN TO THEIR HEADS, THEIR TAILS TO THEIR RUMPS AND EYEBROWS TO THEIR SKULLS.

THIS INSULT ENRAGED MATHOLWCH, BUT HE WAS SATISFIED THAT BENDIGEIDFRAN WAS NOT PARTY TO THE EFFRONTERY. HE AGREED TO TAKE FRESH HORSES, A STAFF OF SILVER AND A WIDE GOLDEN VESSEL AS REPARATION.

DESPITE THEIR RESURRECTED AMITY, BENDIGEIDFRAN SENSED THAT MATHOLWCH WAS NOT AS FRATERNAL AS BEFORE OR GRATIFIED BY THE GIFTS OF ATONEMENT.

CONSEQUENTLY THE KING OF THE ISLE OF THE MIGHTY DECIDED TO CROWN HIS REDRESS BY GIVING THE KING OF IRELAND THE REMARKABLE CAULDRON OF REBIRTH.

IF PLACED WITHIN, THIS CAULDRON COULD RETURN DEAD WARRIORS TO LIFE – ALTHOUGH THEY WOULD BE REBORN MUTE.

WITH THIS COMPENSATION FOR THE INIQUITOUS DEED, THE FESTIVITIES CONTINUED UNTIL BRANWEN AND MATHOLWCH SAILED FOR IRELAND.

ONE YEAR LATER, BRANWEN GAVE BIRTH TO A HANDSOME BOY CALLED **GWERN**.

BUT THERE WERE THOSE AMONGST THE KING'S RETINUE WHO REMAINED DISGRUNTLED BY THE DISFIGUREMENT OF THE HORSES, WITH EFNISIEN'S NAME CURSED FOR MAIMING IRELAND'S FINEST STEEDS.

AS KING, MATHOLWCH WAS WEAK, CONCERNED ONLY WITH HIS STANDING AMONG HIS PEOPLE. HE CONSEQUENTLY AGREED TO TAKE REVENGE FOR THE CALUMNY.

MATHOLWCH DECIDED TO BANISH BRANWEN FROM HIS SUMPTUOUS COURT, TO WORK AS A KITCHEN MAID AND TO SUFFER DAILY BEATINGS BY THE BUTCHER.

Such was Branwen's unending torment that she decided to tell her brother of her mistreatment. She sent him a message tied to a tamed starling.

The brave starling flew across the waves and found the king at court in CAER SAINT in ARFON.

Furious at the letter, Bendigeidfran decided immediately to release his sister from her strife.

Leaving his son CARADOG to rule in his absence, Bendigeidfran and his men headed for Ireland – the soldiers in ships, the king striding through the waves.

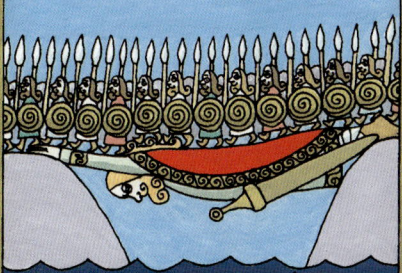

In his own defence, Matholwch destroyed the only bridge across the LLINON, the mysterious river which could swallow anything that dared sail its waters.

"Let he who leads be a bridge!" exclaimed Bendigeidfran, dashing Matholwch's vantage. He lay across the river from one bank to the other, his army marching over his back.

A fearful Matholwch knew Bendigeidfran was renowned as an indomitable warrior.

He decided to abdicate the throne to his son Gwern – but despite receiving this news, the king of the Brythons was not pleased.

Matholwch again called his counsellors. They advised him to yield the kingdom of Ireland to Bendigeidfran, and to pay him dutiful homage for the rest of his days.

They also advised him to construct a high and mighty hall as never before seen – a hall large enough to shelter Bendigeidfran and all his men, as well as Matholwch and his own retinue.

This proposal was conveyed to Bendigeidfran. With his beloved sister Branwen in tears, begging him to accept for the sake of Ireland, he agreed.

The Irish proceeded to build this magnificent hall taller, wider, finer and more luxurious than any other hall ever built before, its roof supported by one hundred pillars.

At dawn on the day Bendigeidfran was to be received at the hall, Efnisien entered, his bitter eyes darting wildly about the place.

He noticed sacks hanging from each of the one hundred pillars. He asked an Irish servant what these sacks contained and was told they held flour.

But Efnisien touched the nearest sack and felt a man's head inside.

He pressed hard until his fingers crushed through the skull and brain of the man in the sack.

He proceeded from one sack to the next, crushing every head until it was dead. These were soldiers ready to fall upon Bendigeidfran and kill him at night. Though helmeted, the soldier in the last sack did not escape the deadly grasp of the king's half-brother.

WITH MATHOLWCH'S PLOT FOILED, BOTH KINGS AND THEIR MEN ASSEMBLED BENEATH THE SAME ROOF TO CELEBRATE GWERN'S ACCESSION TO THE THRONE OF IRELAND.

BUT AMID THE FESTIVITY, ANGER ENGULFED EFNISIEN YET AGAIN, JEALOUS OF GWERN IN THE ARMS OF NISIEN AND MANAWYDAN. HE TOOK THE CHILD BY HIS FOOT AND THREW HIM INTO THE FIRE.

FACED WITH THIS ATROCIOUS ACT, MATHOLWCH'S ENTOURAGE DREW THEIR SWORDS AND CAUSED A BLOODY CALAMITY.

THE CYMRY BRAVELY DEFENDED THEMSELVES, BUT IN NO TIME THE IRISH BEGAN TO OVERCOME, TURNING TO THE CAULDRON OF REBIRTH TO RESURRECT THEIR DEAD.

EFNISIEN REALIZED THAT THE RESPONSIBILITY FOR THIS CALAMITY WAS HIS, AND WENT TO LIE AMONG THE IRISH DEAD TO BE THROWN INTO THE CAULDRON OF REBIRTH.

HE WAS THROWN INTO THE CAULDRON, WHERE HE STRETCHED AND PUSHED, BREAKING THE CAULDRON INTO FOUR PARTS.

THROUGH HIS EFFORTS, EFNISIEN DIED, HIS HEART BROKEN.

A FURIOUS BENDIGEIDFRAN TURNED ON MATHOLWCH AND KILLED HIM. WITH THIS, THE IRISH FLED THE FIGHTING.

THE CYMRY WERE VICTORIOUS, BUT PAID A DEAR PRICE. ONLY SEVEN OF THEM REMAINED ALIVE, AMONG THEM BENDIGEIDFRAN, FATALLY WOUNDED BY A POISONED LANCE.

BEFORE DYING, THE KING TOLD HIS MEN TO STRIKE OFF HIS HEAD, AND AFTER SEVEN YEARS OF FEASTING AT HARLECH, TO TAKE IT TO GWALES IN PENFRO.

THERE THEY SHOULD STAY IN A GREAT HALL FOR FOUR SCORE YEARS, HIS HEAD AS CONVIVIAL AS EVER DURING THAT TIME, WITHOUT SORROW OR GRIEF TO TROUBLE THEM.

BUT ONCE THE DOOR WOULD BE OPENED ON ABER HENFELEN, IT WOULD BE TIME FOR THEM TO TRAVEL TO THE GWYNFRYN, THERE TO BURY THE HEAD FACING THE SEA TO PROTECT BRITAIN FOR ETERNITY FROM INVADING OPPRESSORS.

ACCOMPANIED BY THE HEAD OF BENDIGEIDFRAN, THE CYMRY WITHDREW FROM IRELAND.

UPON THEIR RETURN TO MÔN AT TALEBOLION, BRANWEN GAVE UP HER LIFE OF A BROKEN HEART, AND WAS THERE INTERRED ON THE BANKS OF AFON ALAW.

FOR SEVEN YEARS THE CYMRY FEASTED AT HARLECH BEFORE WITHDRAWING TO THE ISLAND OF GWALES. THERE THEY FOUND A MIGHTY HALL HIGH ABOVE THE SEA, WITH TWO DOORS OPEN, AND ONE CLOSED.

AFTER FOUR SCORE YEARS OF CELEBRATING THE FEAST OF THE WONDROUS HEAD, HEILYN SON OF GWYN VENTURED TO OPEN THE CLOSED DOOR. IN SO DOING ALL THE GRIEF AND SORROW OF THE INTERVENING YEARS BECAME KNOWN TO THEM.

THENCEFORTH THEY WERE UNABLE TO REMAIN AT GWALES AND IMMEDIATELY WITHDREW TO THE GWYNFRYN TO BURY THE HEAD OF BENDIGEIDFRAN, WHO WOULD FROM THAT TIME PROTECT THE ISLAND OF BRITAIN.

AN INTERESTING TALE, MY FAIR BARD... BUT WHAT SHOULD I LEARN FROM IT?

LEARN WHAT YOU WILL! IT IS NOT FOR ME TO SAY...

TAKE THIS RING AS A TOKEN FOR YOUR STORY. IT IS SCANT REWARD FOR THE LESSON.

PLEASE, NO! KEEP IT! MY REWARD WILL BE FOR YOU TO CONSIDER BENDIGEIDFRAN'S DEEDS – HOW HE REINED HIS ANGER, AND HOW HE GAVE PEACE AND FORGIVENESS TIME TO GROW.

WITH THOSE WORDS THE YOUNG MAN DISAPPEARED INTO THE NIGHT, LEAVING ARTHUR TO PONDER HIS MESSAGE.

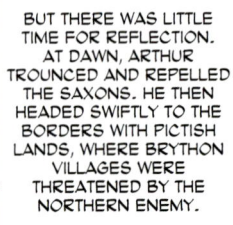

IN THE MEANTIME, FAR FROM THE BATTLEFIELD...

GOOD DAY, MORGEN!

MY CHILD, YOU HAVE INDEED LEARNED MUCH OF THE ANCIENT LORE...

...BUT TO PREVAIL OVER AN OLD SAGE LIKE ME THERE IS YET MORE TO LEARN.

YOU'RE NOT OLD!

DON'T FOOL YOURSELF! MY COUNTENANCE MAY NOT BE RAVAGED BY TIME – BUT INSIDE, MY BODY PERISHES JUST AS A WITHERING TREE...

MYRDDIN STAYED AWHILE WITH THE DELIGHTFUL MORGEN.

HE GAVE OF HIS KNOWLEDGE WITHOUT ONCE RESPONDING TO HER QUESTIONS. IT WAS HE WHO WOULD DECIDE WHAT SHE WAS TOLD AND WHAT WENT UNTOLD.

THE MAIDEN FOLLOWED HIS INSTRUCTION. SHE LEARNED THAT THE ELM TREE BORE DREAMS AND SLUMBER; THE HAWTHORN BORE SUCCOUR FROM THE SPIRITS OF THE OTHERWORLD; AND THE BEECH OPENED THE WAY TO COMMUNE WITH THE ANCIENTS OF OLD.

SHE LEARNED THAT THE FUTURE COULD NOT BE SEEN WITHOUT COMBINING THE POWERS OF THE HAZEL AND THE WILLOW; THAT THE POPLAR WAS CONSECRATED TO THE FALLEN DEAD; AND THAT FERN SPORES COULD RENDER A MAN INVISIBLE.

AS AN OBEDIENT PUPIL, MORGEN ABSORBED HER INSTRUCTION, HER TEACHER AMAZED BY HER ABILITY.

BUT MYRDDIN COULD NOT STEM HER CURIOSITY AND ENTHUSIASM. HE WOULD TURN SILENT WHEN MORGEN STROVE TO LEARN TOO MUCH.

THE OBJECTIVE FOR ARTHUR AND HYWEL HAD YET TO BE REALIZED...

NOT CONTENT WITH THEIR VICTORY, THEY ADVANCED DEEP INTO PICTISH TERRITORY, ANNIHILATING THE RUMP OF THE ENEMY ARMY.

ARTHUR WAS INTENT ON EXTERMINATING THE THREAT POSED BY THESE WARLIKE TRIBES ON THEIR NEIGHBOURING BRYTHONS.

WEARILY THE PICTS RETREATED NORTH TO THE HEART OF THEIR LANDS, AND CAME TO A LAKE...

SIXTY STREAMS AND RIVERS FLOWED INTO THIS LAKE, WHICH CONTAINED SIXTY ROCKY ISLETS AFFORDING SIXTY REFUGES FOR THE PICTS.

AWARE THAT THE MIGHT OF ARMS WOULD PROVE FRUITLESS IN EXPELLING THE PICTS, ARTHUR DECIDED TO BLOCKADE THE LAKE.

HIS PLAN WAS SIMPLE. TO WAIT UNTIL THE ENEMY STARVED.

HYWEL... TELL ME ABOUT THE SIXTY ISLETS IN THIS LAKE, AND THE ROCKY OUTCROP ON EACH ONE...

THIS IS LLUMONWY, ONE OF THE THREE FABLED LAKES OF BRITAIN.

EACH OUTCROP ON EACH ROCKY ISLET HARBOURS AN EAGLE'S NEST.

WHEN THE EAGLES GATHER ON A SINGLE OUTCROP TO CRY IN UNISON, THEN BRITAIN WILL FACE MISFORTUNE.

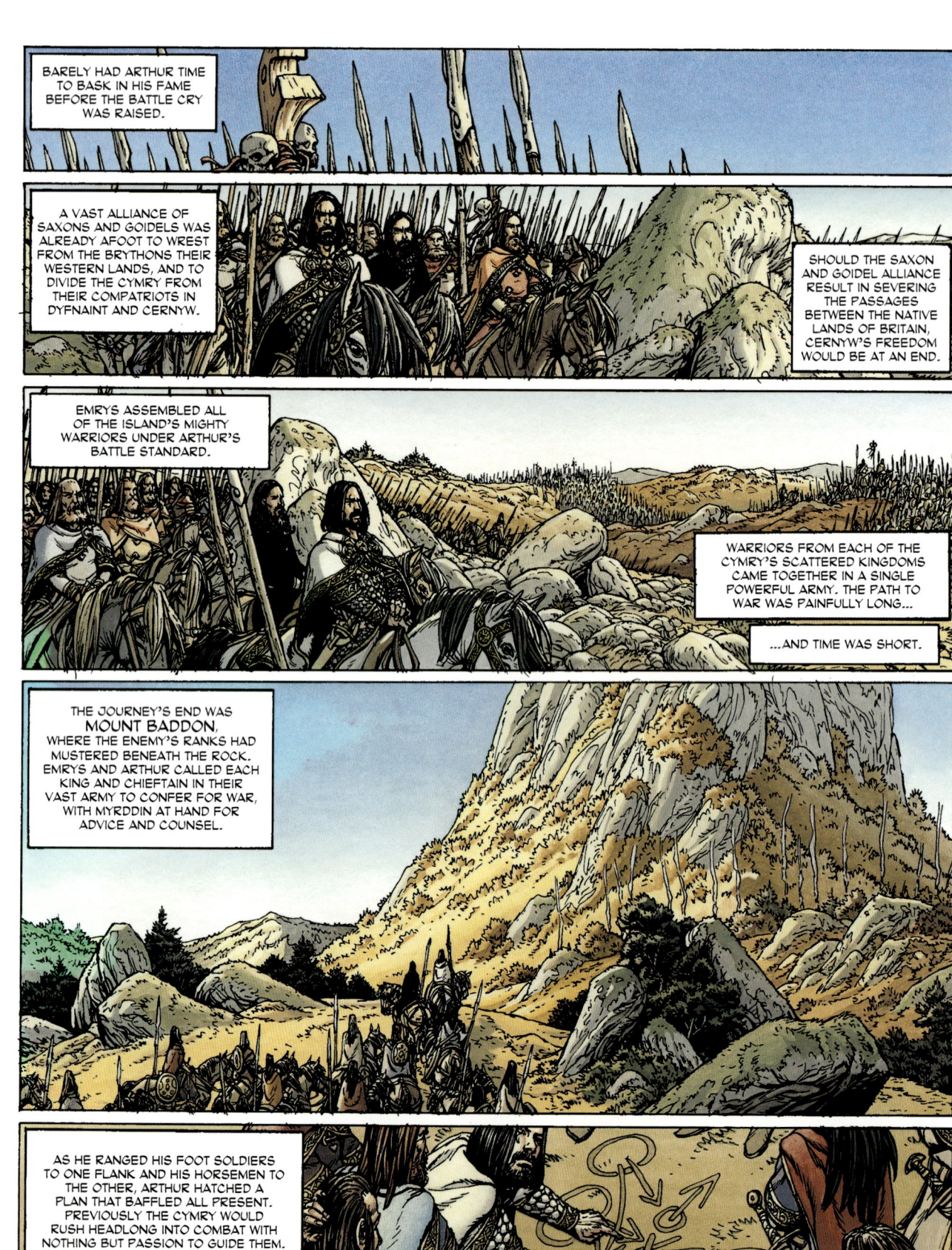

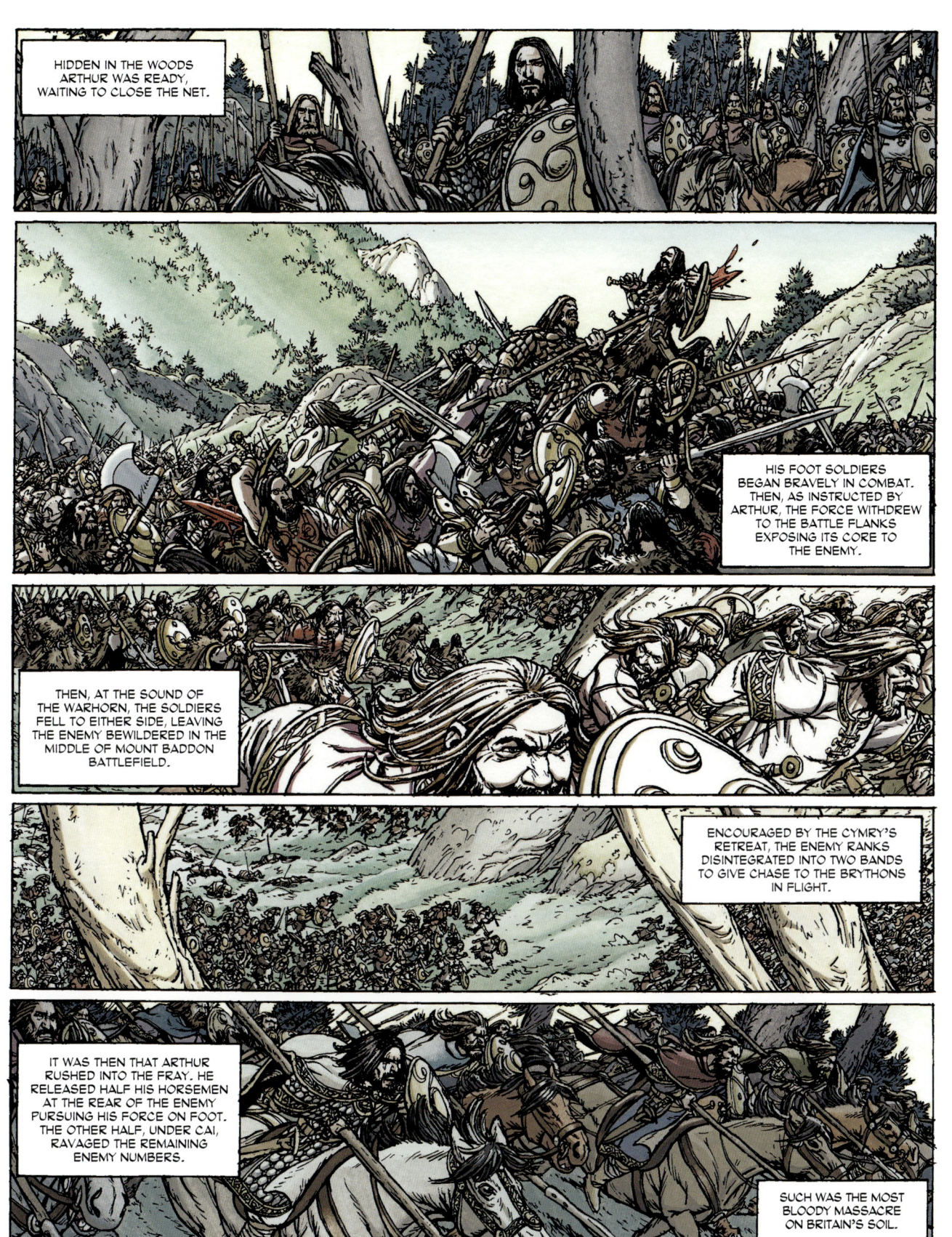

Although Cai and Bedwyr and many others excelled in bravery that day, none was as resolute as Arthur.

Astride his white horse, LLAMRI, the leader of the Brythons descended on the mêlée. Beneath his horse's heavy hooves, many of the enemy lay dying.

At his waist, his knife CARNWENNAN.

He was cloaked by his magic cape GWEN.

RHONGOMYNIAD, his lance, in his hand.

WYNEBWRTHUCHER, his shield, on his shoulder.

Extinguishing Saxon and Goidel, one after another, none who faced him could not feel fear in the final instant of life.

When his lance became blunt he drew CALEDFWLCH from its sheath — encouraging the Cymry ever more as the deadly blade rained down on the enemy.

It is said of Arthur that he killed over 960 of his enemy that day — and that he, more than anyone else, was responsible for the victory at Mount Baddon — as King Emrys overlooked the battle from his vantage point above.

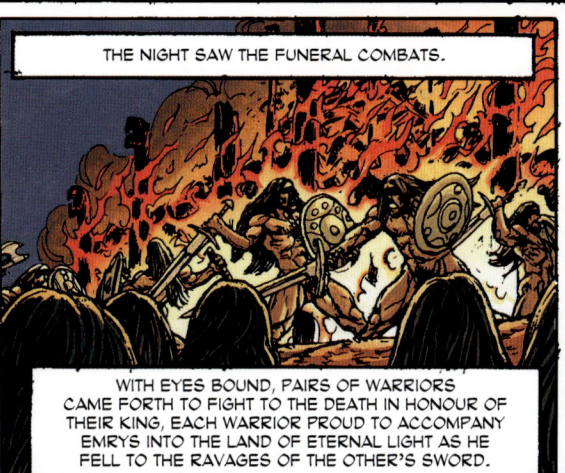

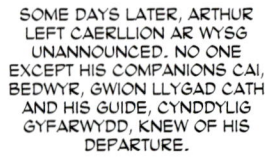

TO FOLLOW

BOOK 3
GWALCHMAI

BOOK 4
CULHWCH AND OLWEN

BOOK 5
TRYSTAN AND ESYLLT

BOOK 6
GERAINT AND ENID

BOOK 7
PEREDUR

BOOK 8
GWENHWYFAR

BOOK 9
MEDRAWD

PRONUNCIATION

Readers unfamiliar with Celtic languages may find themselves mildly baffled by the Arthurian character and place names presented in this book. Rather than yield to possibly more familiar forms of personal names of later Arthurian romance, the names found in the Welsh Arthurian tradition have been retained, names which were echoed in the later Medieval works of writers such as Geoffrey of Monmouth and Chrétien de Troyes. These are presented in modern Welsh orthography, and the following guide may assist in their correct pronunciation and interpretation. Welsh is a phonetic language, so every letter in a word is pronounced. However the Welsh alphabet of 28 characters contains some double letters, which, when combined, have their own sounds. Welsh pronunciation is not harsh; rather, the spoken language is soft and rhythmic, with the accent normally on the penultimate syllable.

A as in '**a**ttack', never as in '**a**cre'.

B as pronounced in English.

C as in '**k**elp', never as in '**c**ereal'.

Ch does not exist in English, but is pronounced as a vocal 'C' in the back of throat, as in a Scottish 'lo**ch**'. Never as in '**ch**urch' or '**ch**ivalry'.

D as pronounced in English.

Dd as in English '**th**is', never as in '**th**in'.

E as in '**e**ver', never as in 'b**e**cause'.

F as in 'o**f**', never as in 'o**ff**er'.

Ff as in 'o**ff**er'.

G hard as in '**g**o', never soft as in '**g**el'.

Ng as in 'bi**ng**'.

H as pronounced in English, but never dropped.

I as in '**i**t', never as in 't**i**me'.

L as pronounced in English.

Ll unique in European languages to Welsh; place your tongue to pronounce 'l', then blow.

M as pronounced in English.

N as pronounced in English.

O as in 'h**o**t', never as in '**o**nly'.

P as pronounced in English.

Ph as in 'o**ff**er'.

R as in 'p**r**ize', but rolled.

Rh as for 'r' but combined with a light 'h'.

S as pronounced in English.

T as pronounced in English.

Th as in '**th**in', never as in '**th**is'.

U as in 'b**ee**', never as in '**u**nion' or '**u**nder'.

W as in 'z**oo**'.

Y short 'uh' as in 'c**u**p', but can also be long as in 'b**ee**' or short as in 's**i**t'.